Please return or renew this item by the last date shown. You may return items to any East Sussex Library. You may renew books by telephone or the internet.

0345 60 80 195 for renewals
0345 60 80 196 for enquiries

**Library and Information Services
eastsussex.gov.uk/libraries**

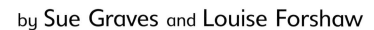

by Sue Graves and Louise Forshaw

W

04507878

I made a big car.

I made a big ship.

I made a big table.

I made a big shop.

I made a big house.

I made a big castle.

I made a big monster.

I made a big chair.

I made a big bed.

Story trail

Start at the beginning of the story trail. Ask your child to retell the story in their own words, pointing to each picture in turn to recall the sequence of events.

Start

Independent Reading

This series is designed to provide an opportunity for your child to read on their own. These notes are written for you to help your child choose a book and to read it independently.

In school, your child's teacher will often be using reading books which have been banded to support the process of learning to read. Use the book band colour your child is reading in school to help you make a good choice. *The Big Box* is a good choice for children reading at Pink 1b in their classroom to read independently.

The aim of independent reading is to read this book with ease, so that your child enjoys the story and relates it to their own experiences.

About the book

In this story, a little imagination turns a big box into all sorts of things to play with.

Before reading

Help your child to learn how to make good choices by asking:
"Why did you choose this book? Why do you think you will enjoy it?"
Support your child to think about what they already know about the story context. Look at the cover together and ask: "What do you think the story will be about?" Read the title aloud and ask: "What could she make the big box into?"
Remind your child that they can try to sound out the letters to make a word if they get stuck.
Decide together whether your child will read the story independently or read it aloud to you. When books are short, as at Pink 1b, your child may wish to do both!

During reading

If reading aloud, support your child if they hesitate or ask for help by telling the word. Remind your child of what they know and what they can do independently.

If reading to themselves, remind your child that they can come and ask for your help if stuck.

After reading:

Support comprehension by asking your child to tell you about the story. Help your child think about the messages in the book that go beyond the story. Ask: "Can you think of any other things the big box might be turned into? Why do you think the girl uses it as a bed at the end of the story?"

Give your child a chance to respond to the story: "Did you have a favourite part? What would you like to use the big box for?"

Use the story trail to encourage your child to retell the story in the right sequence, in their own words.

Extending learning

Help your child extend the story structure by using the same sentence pattern and adding some more elements: "A big bed could help us pretend to be in different places. I made a big forest. Now you think of one."

On a few of the pages, check your child can finger point accurately by asking them to show you how they kept their place in the print by tracking from word to word.

Help your child to use letter information by asking them to find the interest word on each page by using the first letter. For example: "Which word is 'monster'? How do you know it is that word?"

Franklin Watts
First published in Great Britain in 2017
by The Watts Publishing Group

Series Editors: Jackie Hamley and Melanie Palmer
Series Advisors: Dr Sue Bodman and Glen Franklin
Series Designer: Peter Scoulding

A CIP catalogue record for this book is
available from the British Library.

ISBN 978 1 4451 5413 8 (hbk)
ISBN 978 1 4451 5414 5 (pbk)

Printed in China

Franklin Watts
An imprint of
Hachette Children's Group
Part of The Watts Publishing Group
Carmelite House
50 Victoria Embankment
London EC4Y 0DZ

An Hachette UK Company
www.hachette.co.uk

www.franklinwatts.co.uk

FSC
www.fsc.org
MIX
Paper from
responsible sources
FSC® C104740